TUTU

Audrey Chevance

DUTTON CHILDREN'S BOOKS   NEW YORK

to Willy Burmann
for his wonderful ballet classes

Y̲our balance is on your standing leg, girls, with your weight over your toes," the ballet teacher reminded his class. "On your *left* leg, Isabelle. Put your mind on the combination, too."

Isabelle Warren sighed. She had been taking ballet for three years, and loved to jump and turn and balance. She tried her best to pay attention in class, but today her mind was on her appointment at the ballet costume shop. In less than an hour she was going to try on her first real tutu. It was the costume she would wear when she and her classmates danced in a new ballet with a professional ballet company.

Isabelle had visited the costume shop last year, when she danced in The Nutcracker. Her party dress had to be remade, because its velvet skirt was worn out and its petticoats ripped from being performed in year after year by different young dancers.

Isabelle had liked the new dress with its soft, heavy skirt and crisp white petticoats, even though it made her hot under the bright stage lights. But she didn't feel like a ballerina in it. From the wings she had watched the older dancers, so light and graceful in their frilly tutus and satin pointe shoes.

After class, Isabelle hurried to an old gray building a few blocks
away and took the elevator to the top floor. She loved the feeling
of stepping into the large, airy costume shop, where something to
dance in peeked out of every corner. Long, gauzy skirts; silk and
satin gowns; shirts and jackets for the men. And tutus were every-
where—snowy tutus, tutus like pastel powder puffs, short Classical

tutus, and long Romantic ones; tutus adorned with sequins, jewels, ribbons, piping, and lace. Newly finished tutus were hung upside down to keep their fullness and shape.

"Hello, Isabelle," said Holly, the director of the costume shop. "Come on in. Your tutu is all ready for you in the fitting room."

Isabelle followed Holly past men and women busy working.

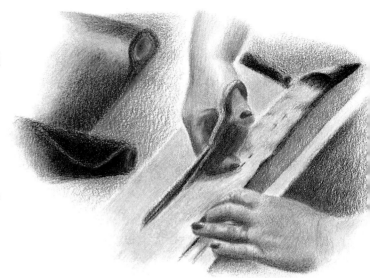

There were dressmakers to cut the fabric;

seamstresses to sew the pieces together, by machine and by hand;

tailors to cut, sew, and fit the men's costumes. In the costume shop men worked on the men's costumes and women worked on the women's.

There were dyers to dye fabric, leotards, tights, unitards, shoes, gloves, buttons, feathers, furs, flowers, and even pearls.

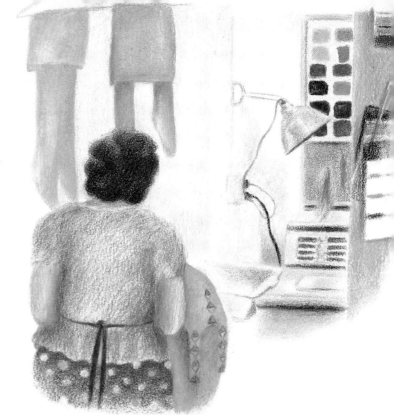

Isabelle passed someone ironing. In the costume shop, everyone ironed and everything got ironed—even feathers—piece by piece, so that costumes stayed neat while being made.

Celina, the millinery lady, sat at a table sewing. She created crowns, hats, flowers, tiaras, and anything else that could be worn on a dancer's head.

Standing in a small fitting room filled with costumes, Isabelle remembered how surprised she had been last week. A fitter named Natasha had already taken her measurements, and Holly had called Isabelle in to try something on. But it had turned out to be nothing more than a stiff waistband.

"This is my tutu?" Isabelle had asked.

"Don't worry," replied Katya, one of the Russian seamstresses. "We are many people here. After forty hour, work hard, tutu will be very pretty."

Now Isabelle studied the costumes on the racks. One, smaller than the rest, was a fluffy pink tutu with velvet petals.

"Is that one mine?" she asked.

"It certainly is," replied Holly. She took the tutu down from the rack. "You see? Your name is here on a label sewn to the waistband."

Isabelle quickly got undressed. She couldn't wait to try on the tutu. It wasn't one stretchy garment like the leotards she had to wear in ballet class or the tutu she had received for her birthday several years ago. It was a professional tutu made of many different pieces, all sewn together.

On top there was a satin bodice sewn to the waistband of the ruffled skirt. Beneath the skirt, there were ruffled underpants, called knickers, which were also sewn to the waistband.

Holly held the tutu off the floor while Isabelle carefully stepped into the knickers. Then Holly pulled the tutu up and Isabelle slipped her arms through the elastic shoulder straps of the bodice. The straps were hidden by velvet petals and little satin flowers.

Isabelle looked at herself in the mirror. Her tutu was so pretty and delicate that even with her socks on, she felt changed and special.

"Oh, it's beautiful!" she said. "It feels so dressy." She lifted the ruffles of the skirt and watched them float down again.

"Stand still while I snap the skirt together and hook the waistband," Holly told her. "Good, the fit is perfect. If the waistband were loose, your tutu would shift every time you moved."

Isabelle's back was not very broad, so Holly fastened the hooks to the farthest row of loops. "I have to get my tape measure from the other fitting room," she said. "Do a couple of *passés* to see how your knickers feel, and I'll be right back."

Isabelle patted the skirt of her tutu. It was trimmed with satin flowers and sparkling rhinestones. This tutu was made just for me, she thought. I'm the very first person to wear it.

Isabelle stood up very straight. "Pay attention!" she scolded herself, imitating her teacher. "Now that we are wearing a tutu, the audience can see every step we take. So we should try not to make any mistakes!"

"*Passé* is a movement. Bring your toes to you. Higher, higher," she said. "Point all five toes, please. Pass through to a tight fifth position and feel long and neat like an asparagus stalk!"

"Make your movements more generous, girls," Isabelle could hear her teacher say. "I know it's not Christmas yet, but as dancers we are supposed to be giving all the time."

Isabelle gave a very generous curtsy. Then she took a candy from the bowl on the table.

Suddenly she heard someone nearby say, "The elastic on the right leg is a little tight."

Following the voice, Isabelle tiptoed across the hall and peeked through a curtain.

"We fix," Katya was saying.

"And then you'll have to come back later in the week to make sure it's all right," Holly added.

Lili, a company ballerina who had danced the Sugar Plum Fairy in The Nutcracker, was standing in a T-shirt and tutu skirt, talking with Katya and Holly. After one of the performances, Lili had autographed her pointe shoes and given them to Isabelle.

"I'll be with you in a minute, Isabelle," said Holly.

"I don't mind if you watch," Lili offered.

Isabelle found room on a table beneath some hanging tutus and sat down to watch. Lili's tutu skirt was covered with lace and pearls, and it had a stiff shape. "Lili's tutu *really* sticks out," Isabelle said quietly. Suddenly her own tutu seemed to droop.

"Lili's tutu skirt was meant to stick straight out and look razor-sharp," said Holly. "It is a ballerina's tutu, so it must make her look regal and elegant. We used seven layers of stiff net for Lili's skirt. Your tutu skirt was specially made with seven layers of tulle, a soft mesh, to give it a gentle shape."

"You are child, dear," said Katya. "Different tutu. Your tutu soft, like bell. Beautiful."

"You know, our costume designer designs tutus in all different styles," explained Holly. "She gets her ideas from many things, especially the colors and shapes of flowers."

Lili was helped into the bodice of her tutu.

"Oh, you look like a princess!" Isabelle said.

"Thank you," replied Lili. "I think you look like a rosebud in your tutu. And that is just as nice."

Lili leaned backward to test the fit of her bodice. She had to be certain that the front would move with her when she did the same *port de bras* onstage. Because her tutu still needed work, there were pins now where there would later be hooks and eyes or snaps and stitching. The bodice would be attached to the waistband in such a way that there would be some "give" when Lili moved.

"The bodice of Lili's tutu is made of velvet and upholstery brocade," said Holly, "the same material that covers chairs and sofas. The bodice has to be very strong, because that's where Lili's partner will hold her and lift her. But it has to be comfortable, too. It's lined with cotton, to protect the fabric and to keep sweat from showing through. And there are even flexible metal 'bones' inside that make the bodice so sturdy it can stand up on its own."

"A lot of dancers sneak the bones out," said Lili. "I keep them in because I don't want the bodice to look baggy. Our choreographer always says that a ballerina must feel special onstage. Her costume should help her feel that way."

"Come on now, Isabelle," Holly said. "It's your turn."

Back in the small fitting room, a few of the women who had worked on Isabelle's tutu came in to admire it on her.

"I love my tutu," Isabelle told them. "Is there a headpiece?" she asked, having noticed Lili's tiara.

"No," answered Holly, "but Celina made these satin flowers for your hair." Natasha draped a length of pink roses around Isabelle's bun.

One of the seamstresses smoothed the neckline in back. "This shouldn't be puckering," she said, marking the spot with chalk. "Otherwise, everything looks fine."

"How does it feel?" Holly asked.

"Great!" Isabelle couldn't help doing a few jumps from her part in the ballet.

"Nothing scratches?"

"The knickers do, a little, but I think that's because I'm not wearing tights."

"Good. Have one last look, and then you'll see it next at the theater."

On the night of the first performance, Isabelle headed down the long stairway that led to the dressing room. It was lined with shiny new pointe shoes standing up to dry. Isabelle loved the smell of the floor polish that the dancers poured into the tips of their shoes to make them harder and last longer. It would be another two years before Isabelle herself could take class in pointe shoes.

Now, for what seemed like the millionth time, she pictured the sequence of steps she had rehearsed over and over. She hummed the music, too. It helped her remember the steps. Her teacher said that if you listen carefully to the music, you put more feeling into your dancing.

In a room beneath the stage, Kristina, the wardrobe mistress, was
helping the girls into their tutus.

Suddenly she cried out, "OH!"

Everyone looked around.

"What do I *see*?" Kristina said to a girl who was letting her tutu

drop to the floor. "We *never* put a costume on the floor! You know better than that, Megan!"

"But I need to go to the bathroom," Megan complained. "So I have to take my tutu off."

"Then hang it up on a hanger. I shouldn't have to remind you."

When all the girls were dressed
and ready, they still had to wait.
So they checked themselves in
the mirror,

or sat, very carefully, and chatted,

or glanced at magazines until it was
time to go upstairs to the stage
level. Their part in the ballet
opened the last act, and then they
appeared again at the very end.

The curtain was still down. Isabelle's friend Emma skipped over to wish her luck. Isabelle felt very excited and a little scared.

Two minutes before the last act began, the stage manager said "Places" over a backstage microphone. Then, just seconds before the curtain rose, he said, "Stand by."

When the curtain went up and the familiar music began, there was no time to be scared. Isabelle concentrated on the steps she had to do, remembering how important it was to dance with all of herself, not just her feet. Her teacher was watching from the wings, and she wanted him to be proud. She listened to the music, mak-

ing her movements large, because she knew she was dancing for the people way up in the fifth ring as much as for those in the first row of the orchestra. Isabelle and her friends smiled when they faced the audience, and when they got a chance, they smiled at one another.

Then, as suddenly as it had begun, it was over.

Isabelle couldn't see the audience, sitting beyond the orchestra pit. But she held her last pose as the applause roared up out of the darkness, amazed by how loud it was. Although she knew she would be performing for two more weeks, she wished the orchestra would start playing so she could dance her part again, right now. She felt light and free and special in her tutu, and the only way to express this was to dance.

A Bit More About Tutus

For elegance and ease of movement, there is nothing quite like a tutu. It is, along with the pointe shoe, the very symbol of the ballerina.

Although costumes with bell-shaped skirts in various forms and lengths date from the seventeenth century, not until 1832, in Paris, when Maria Taglioni wore a long white dress in *La Sylphide*, did the modern Romantic tutu come into being. Called a sylphide and popularized by Taglioni's renown, the costume had a fitted bodice, minimal sleeves, and a soft, misty skirt made from layers of tulle that ended above the ankle.

As ballet technique advanced, the tutu skirt was shortened to reveal the more intricate footwork, until the Classical tutu, with its fluffy, projecting skirt attached to ruffled underpants, freed and exposed the entire leg while concealing, for modesty's sake, the ballerina's bottom. A piece of material separating the waistband from the skirt, called a yoke or basque, was first introduced to make a short Russian ballerina look taller by displaying her waist and hips. Children's tutus do not have yokes.

A Classical tutu skirt is traditionally made with seven ruffled layers of either a soft mesh, giving the skirt a gentle shape, or a very stiff net, causing it to stick straight out. Occasionally a wire hoop may be used, but it is not generally favored by partners. The layers are graduated in length, with the bottommost the shortest. The topmost layer, called the tutu plate, is the longest. The skirt's decorations are sewn to it. To keep the tutu plate from flying up and catching on the ballerina's earrings or on her bodice trimmings, and for general streamlining, threads called tacks are sneaked down through the ruffled layers and maintain the skirt's shape.

It takes about forty hours of care and hard work to make a tutu, not to mention the experience and tradition that lie behind its design. Because a tutu must withstand stress, strain, and sweat, special thread is used, seams are doubled, and stitching, done on industrial machines, is reinforced. The inside of the bodice may be quilt-stitched for extra strength. Only the finest materials are chosen, and care is paid to the tiniest details, even if they cannot be seen by the audience, because the craftsmanship of every aspect of the tutu is a sign of respect for the ballerina and her art, as well as an inspiration to her.

Generally, a tutu is cleaned after three performances. Sometimes the whole tutu is dry-cleaned, although now and then the bodice can simply be spot-cleaned by hand. Most often, workers in the costume shop remove the bodice, tutu plate, and yoke and send these pieces for dry cleaning. The rest of the tutu skirt is dipped by hand in cold water, and when everything is clean, the whole tutu is reassembled. With good care, a tutu can last about twenty performances before it must be completely remade. Ultimately it is the handling that goes with partnering—the holding, lifting, turning, and catching—that most wears out a tutu. Because children are not partnered, their tutus may last for many years.

The word *tutu*, perhaps suggested for the ballet costume by the ruffles that cover the ballerina's *derrière*, is a French nickname for a baby's bottom.

ACKNOWLEDGMENTS

My sincere thanks to Oona Mekas, Kristina Kaiser, Perry Silvey, John Braden, Merrill Ashley, Alexandra Danilova, Tom Kelley, everyone at The New York City Ballet Costume Shop, the young girls at The School of American Ballet, and George Fearon.

I wish I could thank the late Ronnie Bates for teaching me the importance of, and respect for, drawing and painting.

Thank you so much, Holly Hynes, for all your help and patience.

I am very grateful to Donna Brooks, my great and kind editor, fellow Farrell fan, and friend, for making this book happen; and to Peter Martins, without whom the book would still be just an idea. *Tusind tak.*

Library of Congress Cataloging-in-Publication Data
Chevance, Audrey.
Tutu/by Audrey Chevance.
p. cm.
Summary: A young ballerina visits the costume shop to be fitted for her first professional tutu and learns how tutus are made.
ISBN 0-525-44769-5
[1. Ballet dancers—Fiction. 2. Costume—Fiction.] I. Title.
PZ7.C428Tu 1991
[Fic]—dc20 91-3506 CIP AC

Published in the United States by Dutton Children's Books,
a division of Penguin Books USA Inc.
375 Hudson Street, New York, New York 10014
Designer: Meri Shardin Keithley
Printed in Hong Kong by South China Printing Co.
First Edition 10 9 8 7 6 5 4 3 2 1